What Did You Do This Weekend?

The Orange Blossom Nudist Resort, Volume 5

W.E. Sinful

Published by W.E. Sinful, 2017.

WHAT DID YOU DO THIS WEEKEND?

First edition. October 4, 2017.

Copyright © 2017 W.E. Sinful.

ISBN: 979-8227252982

Written by W.E. Sinful.

Table of Contents

What Did You Do This Weekend?

Book 4
From the Orange Blossom Nudist Resort Series

By W.E. Sinful

Thank you for reading

Introduction

The Orange Blossom Nudist Resort series is a fictional series dealing with the sexual adventures of singles and couples at a fictitious nudist resort. The series is not intended to depict the actual nudist lifestyle but to take readers on a sexual fantasy.

'What Did You Do This Weekend?' is the fourth book of the Orange Blossom series. Rachel, a co-worker of Jim's, learns that Jim and his wife Jane have a naked secret, that of being nudists. After overcoming their initial embarrassment of being discovered, Jim and Jane invite Rachel and her husband to the Orange Blossom.

This erotic fantasy has it all, interracial, foursomes, voyeur, orgy, bondage, anal, and more.

Chapter 1 – New Friends

Jim and Jane relaxed in the hot tub at the Orange Blossom Nudist late Saturday night. The 'Bare Assets Band,' at the far side of the pool, could be heard playing their closing song.

"I really enjoy our weekend retreats. I just wish we could spend more time here," Jane said.

The couple across from Jane left, exposing a water jet behind the other couple. Jane parted her thighs slightly and twisted her butt a little so the water jet was directed at her bare crotch. As she did, she leaned back to snuggle closer to Jim as he put his arm around her and gently caressed her exposed tits.

"Jim, the resort is advertising a nude 5k run around the grounds for the fourth of July. The fourth is on a Wednesday, and we both have it off. Do you think we could come back on the fourth and enter?"

"Did you forget Jane? You said you would go to my company's 4th of July picnic. "We can cancel, though. A naked jog around the resort does sound fun."

"I am sorry, I forgot. I haven't met many of your coworkers, and I want to meet them. How about we book a room for the weekend after the 4th? That way, we can go to the picnic, and I can meet your coworkers, and then we can spend two full days here the following weekend. We will try to do the next naked run the Orange Blossom has."

"That's great, and they want to meet you too. I keep using your mother as an excuse for not golfing or fishing with them on the weekends. We spend most of our weekends either here or going to a nude beach, which I definitely don't mind, but they feel like I have deserted them. The women I work with want to meet this super wife of mine, who has me wrapped around her little finger."

"Just tell them you like coming here to the nudist resort. They will understand." Jane said with a chuckle as she let her hand run across his dick.

"Yeah, right, just like you tell your coworker what you do on the weekends."

Just then, a couple that Jim and Jane recognized from dancing with the band played approached the hot tub. They were easy to remember. He was a blue-eyed, blond Nordic type, tall and lean with a chiseled physique. She was tall, long-legged, slender, big-chested, and very ... black. The contrast between his paleness and her blackness couldn't be any starker.

"Mind if we join you?" The man said in a thick foreign accent.

"No, come right in and be our guests," Jim said. "My name is Jim, and this is my wife, Jane."

The man assisted the female into the tub first. Both Jim and Jane could not help but notice how she allowed her legs to splay apart as she entered. It was as if she was giving them a porn magazine-style crotch shot as she awkwardly got into the tub directly across from Jim. Although this was a nudist resort, most female guests would try to be dignified and keep their knees closer together. Jim also couldn't help but notice her ample breasts.

"Thank you. My name is Deshawn, and this is my husband, Denzel." The female said, with a distinctive French accent, as her husband slid in beside her.

"I take it from your accent that you two aren't from around here?" Jim asked as he took another glance at Deshawn's rack.

"Jim, don't be so rude," Jane said, taking notice of not only Jim's comment but him checking out Deshawn's tits.

"That's quite all right," Denzel replied in very broken English. "We typically vacation at naturalist resorts in France, where we are from, but this year, we decided to try an American resort."

"I suspect you're thinking they don't look French," Deshawn said. "My mother was the Cameroon Ambassador to France, and I was born in Paris and have spent most of my life in France. Denzel's father owns a large coffee plantation in Cameroon. We were both attending University in Paris when we met. We have been married for three years and still live in Paris. Denzel is a manager at an electronics company, and I do research work for a pharmaceutical company." Kind of uppity, Jane thought to herself. But that's a thing about nudist resorts. When you first meet someone, it is harder to judge them if they do not have clothes on.

"Where are you two from?" Deshawn asked. "I notice, Jane, that you have a darker skin complexion than your husband."

"Oh, we're just a couple of local American mongrels," Jane said. "We come here most weekends."

"Forgive my wife's bluntness," Denzel said, unsure of his English. "This is our first time in America."

"What do you mean, mongrels?" Denzel asked, still struggling for the right English words.

At least Denzel had some class. Jane thought to herself, and the big guy was also kind of sexy with his French accent. "I just mean Jim and I are typical Americans of mixed heritage. Jim would probably be more tanned, but he smears on the SPF-50 sunblock like he owns stock in the company."

"Hey, I don't want to get skin cancer, okay."

"Well, I'm envious of you two. It must be nice to come to this beautiful place and be clothes-free whenever you want?" Deshawn said, trying to move the conversation on.

"Jane and I enjoy it. We have been into the nudist lifestyle for about a year, and since then, we have made many new friends." Jim said as he glanced at Deshawn's boobs again. This time, all three of the others caught his glances.

"Jim, quit looking at her boobs," Jane quipped, loud enough for Deshawn to hear. "It's not proper nudist etiquette."

"It is all right, Jane. I get a lot of stares from the guys, either because of my boobs or my oversized husband. I also saw Jim checking me out earlier on the dance floor. Although it might have had something to do with me repeatedly backing into him when we were all out on the floor.

Your husband is kind of cute. And Jane, I also saw you checking out my husband."

"Oops, you caught that? Well, there is a lot of Denzel to check out. Tall and good-looking. In short, he is a hot, sexy guy. Besides, I caught him checking me out, too."

"It sounds like we were checking each other out," Denzel said. "Maybe we should all go to our room to check things out a bit closer?"

Jim and Jane quickly accepted the invitation. As they walked to the room, Jim and Deshawn held hands, swinging them back and forth like a couple of kids on a school playground. Their thoughts, however, were not those of little children, as Jim's dick was already starting to rise in anticipation of his next conquest.

Following close behind, Denzel and Jane made their erotic intentions even more apparent. Denzel's had his right hand in the crack of Jan's ass, massaging her left butt cheek, and Jane was holding onto his big stick.

When the door closed, it became apparent this would be a straight partner swap.

Jim and Deshawn were about the same height. They embraced and kissed as Jim used his free right hand to massage Deshawn's Left tit. Jane and Denzel were in a similar clutch. But, the towering Swede had to bend over while Jane stood on her toes for their lips to meet.

The guys weren't wasting much time with formality and wanted to get down to the business of fucking the other guy's wife. Jim quickly broke the kiss and pushed Deshawn back onto the king-size bed with her butt on its edge. Her long legs were spread, and her feet were still on the floor. Jim moved between her legs and bent forward to suck and massage her tits. Denzel had similar desires. Pushing Jane backward slightly and bending down to put an arm behind Jane's knees, he quickly picked up Jane to carry her to the opposite side of the bed, where he laid her on her back. She was in a position similar to Deshawn's, with her legs spread wide on the opposite sides of the king-sized bed. The girl's heads were now next to each other. They turned their heads to face each other and kissed as the men ravished their bodies.

The first thing both men did was attack the women's breasts. Jim massaged Deshawn's gigantic soft melons as he sucked a nipple into his mouth. And Denzel explored Jane's smaller but firmer offering. The girls, for their part, continued to kiss as their tongues explored each other mouths.

Then, as if on cue, both men went down on the girls.

Jim couldn't wait to explore the black pussy. She was cleanly shaven with black protruding lips and a stud pierced through the hood above her clit. Jim first kissed the stud, then licked her outer lips. He then spread her black lips to expose her inner pinkness. On the outside, other than her blackness Deshawn's pussy didn't look much different than his wife's, and the inter-pinkness was the same. Now for a taste test. He stuck his tongue into the depths of her pink twat, as far as he could reach, before pulling back to lick upward across her clit. Jim could help but think how her pussy tasted much different from other pussies he had eaten. It's so different on the outside, but otherwise, it's much the same.

Similarly, Denzel began to explore Jane's tight little pussy.

Like the rest of Denzel, his tongue was also big, filling Jane's twat. Although Jane has had many different men go down on her, few, if any, had a tongue that could reach into her interdeeps as far as Denzel's could. Her hips squirmed in appreciation as she tried to get his tongue further.

The girls continued to French as the guys sucked their pussies. Other than the occasion thrashing of their hips, they seemed oblivious to the tongue lashing they were receiving below.

The guys were now ready to fuck their new conquests. Denzel's dick, giant like the rest of him, stood out rigid and firm like a massive Viking sword prepared to attack. However, before they started fucking, Jane wanted a taste of DeShawn's pussy. The girls crawled to the center of the bed into the '69' position, with Deshawn on top, as they began to lick and suck each other's pussy. This position gave Jim easy access to Deshawn as he came up from behind to fuck her doggy style.

Once Jim was in Deshawn's pussy, there wasn't much room for Jane, so she sucked on her husband's ball sack as his white dick entered the black pussy. It was now Denzel's turn to get in on the action. Deshawn assisted him by spreading Jane's pussy lips, inviting her husband to enter Jane's tight little snatch. Although petite, Jane had plenty of experience with big cocks. Jane relaxed as Denzel slowly guided his dick into her waiting hole. Jim was now banging into Deshawn with a rapid tempo, causing his balls to swing back and forth, preventing Jane from continuing to suck on his ball sack. So, she reached up and massaged Deshawn's clit, as her husband's dick thrust in and out, just above her fingertips.

Jim and Deshawn were getting into a good rhythm, but Jane and Denzel had problems. Because Denzel was so tall and Jane so far up in the center of the bed, he had to bend his knees uncomfortably and struggle to keep his dick in Jane's pussy. It wasn't working for Denzel and Jane, with the four arranged like that.

Denzel grabbed Jane's legs behind her knees and pulled her out from under his wife. Then he picked Jane up like a little girl and lowered her down on his dick in a standing position. Jane guided Denzel's dick into her pussy as she wrapped her legs around his waist.

Once his big dick was entirely up her twat, Jane wrapped her arms around Denzel's neck to hold on. Denzel put his large hands under her butt cheeks to raise her up and down on his dick as he began to fuck her like she was a fuck toy.

Over on the other bed, Deshawn and Jim were still going at it doggie style, making loud slapping sounds each time Jim slammed into Deshawn's ass. Jim started to moan in anticipation of his pending orgasm. Both Jane and Denzel realized he was about to shoot his load into Deshawn's pussy and slowed their fucking tempo to watch. Jim lurched and bucked as he came. As his orgasm subsided, Jim continued to fuck Deshawn so that she could get off as well. Jane and Denzel could see Jim's glistening white cum seep out of Deshawn's black pussy as Jim continued to thrust. Soon, Deshawn clutched the bedsheets as she came. As Jim pulled out, white cum oozed out of her black pussy and down the dark skin of her leg.

After they came down from their orgasms, it was Jim and Deshawn's turn to watch their spouses fuck. The athletic nature of a standing fuck position delayed Denzel coming, as Jane came first, clutching Denzel tightly as she orgasmed. After that, Jane's body went limp as Denzel continued to bounce his new fuck toy up and down on his dick. Finally, Denzel began to groan, indicating his impending orgasm. Denzel started drilling into her as deep as he possibly could, depositing his load of cum in Jane's tight little cunt. Denzel seemed to freeze. He was motionless except for the pulsing of his balls as his nut sack shot a hot stream of cum into Jane's hungry pussy. After a short pause, he lifted her off his dick. Denzel's dick fell out of Jane's dripping pussy with a plop and was followed by what seemed to be an endless river of cum gushing from her pussy.

After a short rest, they were ready to go at it again. This time the girls started it off by sucking the dick of the other's husband, bringing them both back to fucking stiffness. But first, the girls decided they would compare the guy's equipment, as the girls sat side by side on the edge of the bed, and the guys stood directly in front of them. This seemed only fair to the girls since the guys had previously compared their pussys. Jim was a little embarrassed by this since Denzel clearly had the bigger dick, but Jim was good-natured about it.

As Jane sucked and licked the tender underside of Denzel's giant member, she gently cupped his nut sack in her hands. "Damn, your nuts are as big as your dick," Jane said.

"That's why so much cum poured out of your pussy after he came," Jim said.

Deshawn similarly stopped sucking on Jim's dick to study it more closely. "Well, I think your ivory pole is a perfect size. Not too big and not too small. I especially find sucking and playing with your circumcised dick fun. It doesn't have that loose foreskin as my husband's uncut dick." She said as she jacked it a little and ran her tongue around Jim's protruding crown.

"Don't get to any ideas, Deshawn. I will not let anyone with a knife near my dick," Denzel said. "I think it's time we put our dick to use again." He added.

"I agree," Jim said as he pushed Deshawn backward on the bed and spread her legs, and Denzel did the same with Jane.

"Girls, pull your knees up to your shoulders and keep your legs spread as far apart as you can," Denzel said. "That way, we can get maximum access to your pussies."

The girls readily agreed and quickly assumed the position.

The guys immediately enter the waiting and spread pussies. It didn't take long before Jim and Denzel both deposited another load of cum in the pussy of the other guy's wife.

For the rest of the weekend, the four were Fuck buddies. They danced to the band together and frolicked in the pool, with occasional fuck breaks.

Chapter 2 - The Naked Truth

"Jane, the strawberry parfait you made was awesome, don't you think, Greg?" Rachel asked as she and her husband Greg conversed with Jane at the Fourth of July picnic Jim's company put on. Rachel and Greg had been introduced to Jane earlier as both co-workers of Jim's.

"Yes, it was awesome, Jane," Greg said. "I have already had two."

Jane couldn't help but notice how Greg kept taking short glances at her cleavage. She knew she had a figure many men admired, but her sundress wasn't that low cut, and Jane didn't think she was putting on a show. She felt kind of sorry for Rachel to have a husband with such a wandering eye. Especially since Rachel herself had a figure most women would die for.

"So, you two both work with my husband?"

"Yes, but not in the same department," Rachel responded. "I work in sales with your husband, and Greg works in accounting."

"Oh yes," Jane responded. "Now I remember, you're my husband's golf partner in your company's golf league."

"Well, I used to be," Greg replied. "You have him so tied up on the weekends, so all I do now is sit at home and watch golf on TV. You stole my golf partner."

"Greg!" Rachel quickly responded and gave her husband a jab with her elbow. "There is nothing wrong with a guy spending time with his wife. You should try it."

"Now, look at what your husband has done," Greg said jokingly. "His time with you has not only cost me a golf partner but got me in trouble with the wife. Speaking of spending time with you, he talks a lot about your mother. How is she doing?"

"She is doing fine. She and her new boyfriend just got back from another cruise. Since retiring, she has hardly ever been home. My mom and her boyfriend have gone on more cruises than I can count."

"Aw ... Jim said she was in the hospital?"

"Well ... My mom was there briefly, and she's... all better now." Jane said with a panic as she realized Jim was using her mother as an excuse for their weekend getaways to the nudist resort."

"I know Jim said she was recovering nicely. But I can't believe the Hospital would release her and permit her to go on a cruise right after a hip replacement?"

"Well... well... My mom is a strong woman."

"Jim, come here," Rachel said loud enough to be heard from a distance as she motioned him to come over.

Jane gave her unsuspecting husband some strange looks as he walked over and didn't know how to warn Jim about the conversation he was about to walk in on.

"Jim, you always use your mother-in-law as an excuse why you can't golf with any of us at the office on the weekend. But you and your wife's excuses don't match. Your wife said she was on a cruise, and you said she was in the Hospital. Tell us the truth."

"I ... was mistaken. Jane's mother was already out of the hospital, and Jane and I went to the movies instead."

"What movie did you see?"

"Look ... I didn't want to be rude, Rachel. I just wanted to spend some time with my wife! Is that OK?"

"Excuse me." Jane interrupted. "I can attest. Jim and I were together overnight by Orlando, although not with his mother."

"Well, you're a lucky lady, Jane," Rachel said. "Jim always tells us he is spending the weekend with you. I assumed he was going to the hospital, but it sounds like you two are e having a lot more fun. My husband Greg only wants to watch golf or some other sport on TV all weekend."

"Hey, I get stressed out at work all week, and the weekend is my time to unwind!" Greg snapped back.

"I could prance around the house naked, and you wouldn't notice," Rachel said with a sneer.

"So, what fun things did you do this weekend, Jane?" Rachel asked her, continuing to press for details.

"Well... Rachel... I pranced around in front of my husband... naked."

"I thought you said you were in Orlando? ... All weekend?"

"We were."

"Sounds like you had a hot time in a hotel room. So, what did you do outside your room? That is after you put your clothes on." Rachel asked, continuing to pry.

"As I said, pranced around ... naked."

"We also went canoeing," Jim interjected, trying to change the subject.

"Oh, I see," Rachel said, sounding confused.

"We did go canoeing... and we did that naked too," Jane said as Jim covered his face with his hand as if trying to hide.

"What are you two, a couple of exhibitionists?"

"I prefer the term nudist. And by the way, my husband didn't just sit around and watch baseball all weekend. Jim also fucked my brains out."

Jim looked around to see if anyone else had heard his wife. Maybe he could find a hole to hide in.

Rachel and Greg stood motionless, with mouths hanging open and shocked faces.

"Sorry," Jane said. "Since you caught us in our little lie, I just wanted to see if I could get a reaction. However, the naked truth is that Jim and I have memberships to Orlando's Orange Blossom Nudist Resort, which is not far from Orlando. We try to spend as many weekends there as we can. Last weekend, we rented a canoe from the resort and went canoeing at the resort's secluded lake. They also rent standup paddleboards and pontoon boats. The resort also has a beautiful heated pool, tennis courts, walking trails, a restaurant, and a nightclub. You two should try it, and I guarantee you it's a lot more fun than watching TV on the weekends."

"Rachel and Greg," Jim said. "Please keep this our little secret. I don't want word getting around the office on what my wife and I do on the weekends."

"Jim, I wish you weren't so embarrassed," Jane said. "It is something we both enjoy together and brings us together. More couples should try it."

"Jane, you make it sound fantastic," Rachel said. "But don't the guys hit on you, and aren't orgies going on all over the place?"

"The resort has strict rules against improper public behavior and respect for others. However, what guests do in the privacy of their rooms is their own business. I have never received any unwelcome advances nor heard anyone else complain. Other than not wearing clothes, it's a lot like any other resort, laid back and pretty quiet." Jane said, conveniently omitting any reference to their recent tryst with Deshawn and Denzel.

"Going to the resort, with its clothes-free freedom, brings Jim and me closer together. You and your husband Greg should try it."

"I would be too embarrassed, and Greg would gawk at all the other naked women," Rachel said.

"First, it is a clothing-optional resort, and you don't have to get naked if you don't want to," Jane said, conveniently omitting the fact that almost everyone at the resort opted for the Full Monty. "Rachel, you are young, have a killer figure, and gorgeous long blond hair. You have nothing to be ashamed of. At first, you might feel a little embarrassed, but then you realize that others around you are just as naked as you are. Rachel and Jim, you should try it. You will soon find it becomes second nature, and you can do a little sightseeing yourself. However, that part will become secondary for both of you in a short while, as you will start making new friends and seeing people for who they really are. It has also brought Jim and me closer together, and things in the bedroom have improved if you know what I mean."

"Jane, did you have to add that part," Jim said, looking red-faced.

Rachel took notice of Jim's discomfort.

"No need to be embarrassed, Jim," Rachel said. "I see Jane's point. Greg and I seem to be in a rut, and I can see going there would spice things up. However, I'm still unsure I can get naked in front of other people."

"I can see you are interested, Rachel. Because we are full members, the resort gave us coupons to hand out to prospective guests for a free weekend. It also includes overnight accommodations Saturday night, so you will have all day Saturday and Sunday to check the place out. Here, you take one, call the resort, and reserve a room for this Saturday night. Jim and I already have reservations for this weekend, and we would be glad to introduce you to the place and show you around. Wouldn't we, Jim?"

"Sure... that would be great," Jim said. Who was he kidding, he thought to himself. He liked the idea of introducing a new couple to nudism, especially when the female half of the couple was a hot blond.

"I must confess I'm interested," Rachel said. "I dread the thought of spending another weekend watching nonstop baseball. However, Greg would never agree to go to a nudist resort, would you, Greg?"

"Well... Rachel, it's not something I would have ever thought of doing. But... if it's something you want to do instead of watching baseball, we can give it a try. Defiantly a change in our weekend routine." Greg said, choosing his words carefully. Her question was one of those loaded female questions. If he acted too excited, his wife would think he was a pervert. However, who was he kidding? The thought of seeing Jane naked and other women at the resort was a turn-on. He was already starting to get a boner just thinking about it, something he had not had for some time.

"Great!" Jane said before either could change their mind. "We will pick you up Saturday morning. Packing will be easy. All you need are sandals and a smile."

Chapter 3 – Cold Feet

"Are you two ready for a totally new experience?" Jane said as she and her husband picked up Rachel and Greg on Saturday morning.

"Yes... I think we are ready. In addition to the large beach towels you told us to pack, we packed a few clothes, just in case we get cold feet," Rachel said.

They didn't talk much on the way there; when they did, it was about work or some other topic unrelated to the nudist resort they were going to. Rachel and Greg were clearly not at ease. They changed the subject if the conversation dealt with anything mildly risqué, such as something they saw on a TV show or in a movie.

Just before they got to the resort, Jim stopped at a convenience store and loaded up on snacks and drinks.

"Wow, this place is definitely off the beaten path," Greg said as Jim pulled up to the Orange Blossom entrance gate. "You would never know this was a nudist resort from the road."

As they drove forward and wound around some strategically placed bushes that blocked the view from the road, several fully nude couples came into view. Going by some tennis courts, it was apparent the players had nothing on except shoes and hats.

"I thought this was clothing optional," Rachel said, a bit panicky.

"It is, but it's a warm sunny day, so I guess most have opted for the ..., not option," Jane said. "Rachel, look over to your right. Over there is a guy with his shirt on."

"Well, that makes me feel better, but he has no pants on!" Rachel exclaimed. "His dick is hanging out for everyone to see."

"It makes me feel better," Greg said. "I can see his dick is smaller than mine."

"Boasting, are we?" Rachel said, putting her hand on his crotch.

"Don't do that, or you will give me a boner."

Check-in went quickly, and they were assigned adjacent rooms with interconnecting doors. Each room had two beds.

"First, let's go into our rooms to put away all the drinks and snacks," Jane said. "And open the doors that separate our two rooms."

"I don't know if I can do this, Jane," Rachel said as they entered their rooms. "I am starting to get intimidated about getting naked in front of a bunch of strangers, especially Jim. He is a coworker of mine, and I will have to face him on Monday, which is stressing me out the most. Are you sure you are okay with him seeing me naked?"

"We come here often," Jane said. "You won't be the first female Jim has seen in the buff, nor will you be our first female friend that has come with us. My good friend Debbie has been here plenty of times with us, and it has not been a problem."

Jane opened the doors between the rooms.

"Okay, what now?" Greg asked, avoiding the obvious issue that it was time to strip off their clothes.

"Keep your clothes on for now, and we will take you two on a quick tour of the resort," Jim said.

Greg and Rachel looked at each other with relief and readily agreed.

The first place they went to was the pool area. As they first left their rooms, Greg and Rachel saw some fully nude people and several fully clothed couples. However, it was a different story when they got to the pool.

"Jane, we passed some people back near our room with their clothes on," Rachel said. "But here, everyone is completely naked around the pool, and the pool is packed. Also, why isn't anyone wearing a swimsuit in the pool?"

"Sorry, you must be fully naked to be in the pool, resort rule," Jane said. "Same with the hot tubs. Nor are you allowed to wear underwear as outerwear around the resort. The management considers underwear, especially the sexy kind, flirtatious."

"I can appreciate that last rule," Rachel said. "One other thing I have noticed is that I don't see the guys standing around and gawking at all the naked women, which makes me feel better. But being naked in front of all these people is still intimidating."

"If anything, everyone is looking at us," Greg said.

"That's because we are the only ones here by the pool with clothes on," Jane said. "They probably think we are a bunch of pervs, checking them out. Let's go over by the tennis and volleyball courts. It's hot out today, so there might be less crowded over there."

A slight breeze rustled through the leaves as they walked down the path to the courts.

"This resort is beautiful, Jane, and that breeze feels good on a hot day," Rachel said.

"When you are naked, you will really like how the breeze feels as it caresses every inch of your body," Jane said.

"It does sound tempting," Rachel said. "Oh, look, most of the tennis courts are empty. There are only two other couples, and that couple is leaving. I used to play a lot of tennis in college, and I wish I had brought my tennis racket."

"What's the deal with the showers over there?" Greg asked. "The showers are just out in the open, no doors or anything."

The shower was a sizeable three-sided affair, with a showerhead on each end wall facing each other. The center portion had three large dispensers labeled soap, shampoo, and conditioner.

"After you work up a sweat, you just go over and shower off," Jim said.

As he spoke, the couple that was leaving stepped into the showers to do just that. Greg and Rachel could help but watch as the female washed under her boobs, and the couple washed each other's backs before washing their own private parts.

"Wow, no sweaty clothes as you play, and when you're done, just jump in the shower," Rachel said. "And no sweaty laundry!"

"I bet if we ask at the office, they will have some rackets and balls they can loan out," Jane said.

"You might not want to do that, Jane. When my wife told you she played tennis in college, she left out the part about being on the college's tennis team. I'm sure my wife could take all three of us on and easily whip us."

"Jim and I play every weekend," Jane said. "I think we can hold our own."

"I haven't played much since college, so I'm probably pretty rusty."

"Well, it sounds like fun!" Jane said. "It is something we can do as couples. Guys against the girls!"

"I guess this means we go back to our rooms ... and get out of our clothes," Jim said.

The doors between the two rooms were still open as they entered the rooms.

"The doors between the two rooms are still open," Rachel said. "But, I guess it doesn't matter since we will all be getting naked anyway. Jane, I still do not know how to overcome the fear of being naked in front of your husband."

"I have a plan," Jane said. "I thought about this before we got here, as I suspected that the two of you would have difficulty getting naked in front of others. I know it can be intimidating at first. But trust me, it will be second nature after a short time. My friend Debbie had the same issue the first time she got naked in front of Jim."

"First, there is no sense removing one sock at a time," Jane said as she unbuttoned her blouse. "First, let's get down to our underwear. We have all exposed more skin at the beach. Come on. Everyone get down to your underwear."

Soon, Jane was down her simple white bra and panties, and Jim in his tight-fitting briefs, clearly defining his package. Rachel and Greg were slower. Eventually, Greg let his cargo shorts drop to his ankles, revealing striped boxers. While Greg undressed, Jane couldn't help but notice how his eyes kept darting at her crotch. Rachel was last, removing her jeans to reveal she wore a matching black lace bra and panties.

"Since we won't need these clothes for the rest of the weekend, let's put them and our other stuff away. This will also let us get used to being around each other in our underwear."

After putting things away, Jane asked them to get their beach towels and meet in Rachel's and Greg's room.

"What next, Jane?" Rachel asked as she and Greg stood holding their towels in front of themselves.

"We will all go to the other room, remove our underwear, and wrap ourselves in the towel. You will then return with the towel wrapped around you, holding it in place with one hand and your undergarments in your other hand. Since this is my idea, I will go first."

Jane left and soon returned, holding the remainder of her clothes in her right hand. She was using her left hand to clutch the ends of the towel wrapped around her, under her left shoulder.

"Here are my panties and bra, and I have nothing on underneath the towel, and I will put them over here out of reach. Notice that the corners of the towel are not tucked in, so if I let go, the towel will fall free. Jim, you go next."

Jim did as he was directed and returned in a like manner.

"Who wants to go next?" Jane asked as Greg and Rachel silently looked at each other. "Come on, who will go next? You would think you two were at a swinger's party about to fuck someone else; you're just going to get naked."

Finally, Rachel broke the silence. "I guess since we are married, we can go together. You might have to see me naked, Greg. It's been a while."

After they left, Jane and Jim could hear light whispering coming from the other room. Jim and Jane thought that they were getting cold feet. However, they eventually returned with undergarments in hand. Jane and Jim also saw a bulge under Greg's towel, indicating he had an erection, but they thought it was best not to comment.

"What next?" Greg asked.

"This next step may seem a little childish, but we will do a simultaneous dropping of the towels. First, I want Jim to stand beside Greg, and I will stand across from Greg about an arm's length away. Rachel, you stand by me and across from Jim. Now, Greg, let me hold the corners of your towel together with my free right hand. Greg, you do the same and hold onto my towel. Jim and Rachel, you two do the same."

"We are now holding up each other's towels, and I want everyone to raise their free arm above their heads. That way, you cannot try holding up your towel with your elbow. We will all let go of the towels simultaneously on the count of three."

"One... two... three!"

Their towels fluttered to the floor, revealing all the ladies' charms and the guys' equipment.

Greg's dick was fully erect and standing straight up. Jane and Jim continued to pretend not to notice. Finally, Rachel saw her husband's erection. "Greg... your... dick."

Greg immediately became embarrassed that his dick was not as flaccid as Jim's and covered his stiff member with his hands. "Damn, I'm sorry. I am not used to seeing a beautiful naked woman like your wife, Jim," Greg said.

"Shit!" Rachel snapped. "What about me!" Pointing to her own naked body.

"Well... well... well." Greg stammered.

"It's okay," Jim spoke up. "I had the same problem when we first started coming here, and I would have Jane give me a quick BJ, which would solve the problem. Let's step out, Jane, so that Rachel can attend to business."

"Sounds like a plan," Rachel said, gently rubbing her husband's right ass cheek.

"That's okay," Greg said, as his embarrassment had taken his mind off sex, and his erection had lessened.

"I think you're missing a good opportunity for a blowjob Greg," Jim said.

"Sometimes, I think Jim gets an erection just so I have to suck him off," Jane said.

"Hey, whatever it takes," Jim said as he gave his wife a peck on the cheek.

"Well, if things are under control, Greg, let's head over to the tennis courts," Jane said, heading for the door. "We will go around the back way to avoid the pool. That way, the two of you can get used to being naked around others and save the crowded pool area for last."

Although they took a roundabout way, they still passed many people. Seeing all the women in the resort in their uncovered natural beauty had a noticeable effect on Greg, as his dick was semi-erect most of the time. Not that he didn't have an equally beautiful wife he loved and admired, but guys tend to become complacent with the familiar and crave variety.

Although not having played for a long time, Rachel wasn't too rusty, as she and Jane handily outscored the guys. Besides being out of shape, another problem she had was her big boobs that kept bouncing around unless she used her free hand to keep them still.

"Damn, am I out of shape," Greg said, after the match, as he rubbed his back, "I need to get more exercise. Every muscle in my body is sore, and my back is aching."

"Me too, and next time, I will have to bring a sports bra," Rachel said, massaging the sides of her big tits.

"One advantage of small boobs," Jane said, cupping her breasts with a hand. So, you two already think there might be the next time?" Jane asked.

"Well, it is still too early to tell, but I'm enjoying myself so far. But for me, there might be a next time. How about you, Greg?" Rachel asked.

"It's not what I envisioned, but I have also enjoyed myself. That is, if you don't count the humiliating thrashing you girls gave Jim and me, I definitely want a rematch in the future."

"Let's use the showers and head to the pool to relax," Jim said. "There is also a place that gives massages by the pool to help with those muscles, Greg if they are still open."

They went to Bare Essence Massage first, and Jim looked at the schedule and clock on the wall. "Oh damn, they are closing in 10 minutes, and those are probably their last customers."

"Dang!" Rachel exclaimed. "You can watch them give the massages through this big open window. The customers are just lying there, naked on the table for everyone out here to watch, and those two giving the massages are half-naked. The female has no top, and her tight-fitting shorts couldn't be any smaller."

"The two giving massages are Bruce and Vicki. They are good friends of ours," Jim said. "State law requires that massage workers keep their pants on. This is a nudist resort, so there isn't much need for customer privacy. Maybe they could make time for you two if we asked them."

The four briefly watch Vickie and Bruce give their customers massages through the open window.

"What's the towel for, over the customer's butt?" Rachel asked

"I am unsure if it is a State law or a resort rule." Jane giggled. "Even though those two customers walked in naked as jaybirds, the masseuses are required to keep their customer's privates covered."

Greg knew getting a massage would help his muscle pains from the shellacking in tennis he had just received. However, he also knew he would surely get an erection if he were to be massaged by a half-naked woman. Hell, he was starting to get an erection just watching her work on her current customer. And getting a massage from a guy seemed awkward to him.

His wife was thinking along the same lines, at least the part about a massage relieving their muscle aches. "Greg, honey, I think you should get a massage, and it will help you get a good night's sleep tonight."

"No way am I going to let some guy put his hands all over my naked body."

"Then you take Vicki, and if you are okay with it, can I have Bruce massage me."

"Rachel, don't take this wrong, but you go right ahead and get a massage. I am sure you would enjoy getting a massage from that muscular guy, and he wouldn't try to take advantage of you with all these potential onlookers."

"Greg, waiting until tomorrow won't give you much relief from your aches and pains tonight. We should both get massages."

"Wait a minute. We are all getting ahead of ourselves," Jane said. "Let's take a break and sunbathe in these lounges until they finish with their current customers. When they are done, I will ask them if they have time for two more."

Vicki's and Bruce's customers soon left, and Jane went in while the others stayed out to see if they could fit Rachel and Greg in.

Chapter 4 – Massage with Extras

"Hi Jane! I see you brought a couple of newbies with you. I could tell by their farmer's tans and ... the woody the guy had going on," Vicki added with a slight giggle. "I was hoping you would stop by this weekend. Ellen and Julie of Bare Assets Band caught me earlier and said the band was thinking of throwing one of their parties tonight. I am sure the band would be glad if you brought your friends. The girl is hot, and it looks like that guy's dick would fill a girl's pussy nicely."

"You can tell Julie and Ellen that Jim and I would want to come. But I don't think our friends are ready for that." Jane responded. "The guy's wife has complained to me that her husband hardly pays any attention to her as it is. I know she wants to add a little more exciting sex life, but I don't think she would be ready for what those two kinky sluts are into.

"Well." Bruce chimed in as he closed the drapes. "He is definitely checking out the other ladies. That boner of his won't be going down anytime soon unless he gets some relief."

"Oh, darn," Jane said. "I see your closing. I was hoping you would have time to fit them in. We played tennis earlier, and both were out of shape, complaining about sore muscles and backs. Can you schedule them for the first thing tomorrow?"

"Don't be silly. We can make time for your friends right now." Vicki said with a devious smile.

"Thanks... I think. I'll get our friends."

"Rachel, Greg, and Jim come on in. They said they have time for two more."

"It looks like you are closing?" Greg said, looking at the draped window as they entered.

"Yes, we just closed," Bruce said. "However, Jim and Jane are our good friends, and they said you two were sore from playing tennis earlier. Friends of theirs are friends of ours. My name is Bruce, and this is my wife, Vicki. What are your names."

"I'm Greg, and this is my wife, Rachel."

"Greg, Jane tells me you two had a workout playing tennis earlier. Let's see if we can make things feel better," Vicki said. "Greg, I want you to lay face down on my table over here, and I'll see what I can do to make you feel better.

"Aw... what's the charge for this?" Greg asked.

"No charge for friends of Jane and Jim," Bruce said. "Now, Rachel, you lie down on my table, and I see if I can make that back of yours feel better."

"You two just relax and enjoy your massages," Jane said. "Jim and I will give you a little privacy and relax poolside."

However, Jane and Jim didn't go over to the pool. They knew Vicki and Bruce well and knew they would give them more than the standard massage treatment. Therefore, like anybody honest about their sexual cravings, they peeked through the cracks of the curtain to watch.

As Vicki and Bruce got ready, Greg asked them, "Aren't you going to put those little towels over our butts?"

"No, I wasn't planning on it," Vicki replied. "Since you are not paying customers, the resort rules do not require us to cover you. Do you want a little towel over your butt?"

"No, I was just curious. I am still learning this nudist thing."

"Now that you mention it, since this is a nudist resort and you are not a paying customer, do you mind if I get out of these tight-fitting shorts?"

Vicki asked as she began to undo the belt of her shorts before waiting for an answer.

"No... I guess not." Obviously, Greg didn't mind Vicki getting naked, but how his wife would react was what concerned him.

Vicki was standing no more than a foot in front of Greg as she pulled down the zipper of her shorts, revealing her red bikini panties. Laying on his belly with his head cocked toward Vicki, Greg's head was at the same height as Vicki's crotch, causing him to look directly at her twat. He couldn't look up at Vicki's eyes, but she could see he was looking directly at her crotch, studying the camel toe that her pussy lips made in the thin fabric of the panties. She wiggled her hips to get the tight jean shorts down. Her massive boobs swayed back and forth with each wiggle she did. After stepping out of the shorts, she started to peel her panties away. Greg's stared at Vicki with lustful eyes as he took in her nakedness.

Vicki was very much aware that Greg was staring at her exposed pussy. However, Greg didn't have to worry about his wife catching him gawking. She was facing the other way, in a similar position to Greg's, engrossed in watching Bruce stripping out of his tight-fitting jeans.

Bruce hadn't asked permission, just said, 'Good idea' and followed Vickie's lead. After removing his jeans, the budge in Bruce's briefs barely contained his package. As he pulled down the briefs, his big dick flipped free, inches from Rachel's face. She swallowed hard, resisting the temptation to suck the giant member into her mouth. If that wasn't enough, Bruce spread his thighs slightly and, using one hand, reached between behind his balls to pull them forward, giving his balls and dick a light fluff.

"Aww, the guys like being free," Bruce said, fully aware that Rachel was checking him out.

Vicki and Bruce began the massages As they typically do, starting on their customers' backsides. However, both used a lighter, more sensual touch than usual. After about five minutes, Vickie and Bruce wanted to see how far they could go.

Bruce paid extra attention to Rachel's inner thighs. She responded by spreading her legs slightly to give him better access. Rachel knew it was not right, but it had been long since her husband touched her there. Or anywhere near her crotch, so she didn't resist the desire to allow Bruce to go further. Bruce realized she was allowing him to explore and took immediate advantage. First, he let his fingers explore higher and lightly touched her pussy lips as if it were by accident. "Sorry," he whispered. Rachel's only response was to spread her thighs a little more. Soon, it was time to move further up. As Bruce reached around to get more oil, he deliberately allowed his dick to brush up against the hand she had by her side. Bruce proceeded to drizzle the oil on her butt cheeks allowing it to flow into the crack of her ass. As he massaged the oil in, he continued to test the limits. First, he ran his hand through the crack of her ass and allowed his fingers to brush against her butthole. No protests. Then he let his right hand follow the curvature of her butt, allowing his hand to slide across her pussy lips, reaching all the way to her clit. No protest. He went back down again. This time, he let his middle finger part her lips. Still no protest. Again, this time allowing a finger to dart into her fuck hole. She was wet, not just from the oil. Soon, he was fully finger-fucking her from behind.

Working on a guy's backside, Vicky did not have as many options to explore a guy's genitals. She massaged his inner thighs and brushed up against his ball sack but knew that would not get him where she wanted him to be. Therefore, Vicky decided to focus on his shoulders. First, she spread a liberal amount of oil all over his backside, from his butt to his shoulders. Greg's eyes widened, and his dick stiffened as she ran an oily finger deep between his cheeks and butthole. The pain of his stiffening dick was unbearable. It was trapped beneath him and pointed downward toward his toes. He desperately wanted to make an adjustment and move it to an upward-pointing position but was too embarrassed to do anything.

"My, your muscles are tight from playing tennis," Vicki said as she massaged his shoulders. "How does this feel?" She asked as she rubbed his shoulders.

"I will give you an hour to stop," Greg said as he squirmed and raised his hips a bit, hoping his dick would flip to an upward-pointing position without him having to touch it. Unfortunately, his dick had grown too large and was hopelessly pinned. Unless he made it evident that he had a boner, there was nothing he could do about his pain.

However, Vicki saw his stiff dick pointing below his balls and realized his discomfort as a smile spread across her face. "Here, let me help you raise your hips."

She reached under him, grasped his stiff member, and readjusted it for him as he did.

"My, you have a big boy," Vicki said with a smile.

"I'm sorry," he said with embarrassment.

"Don't be embarrassed. It happens to a lot of guys. Just relax and let your mind drift to wherever it wants to go. I do have a problem, though, with your broad shoulders. It's difficult for me to work on your far shoulder properly." With that, she pushed his legs together and climbed up onto the bottom end of the massage table. She placed both hands on his lower back and pushed upward with maximum force. As she reached his shoulders, she allowed her tits to slide across his backside. At first, she did it lightly and slowly increased the body contact until Greg was receiving a full Nuru massage treatment. There was no question about where Greg's mind was going. His dick began to throb as Vicki's tits slid along his back, and her thighs gripped his butt. He could even feel her love mound sliding across his ass cheeks as she twisted her hips from side to side.

Vicki continued this for several minutes, then looked over at Bruce to see how he was doing. He had two fingers up Rachel's twat and his thumb rubbing her butthole. Rachel had her eyes closed and a dreamy look on her face, obviously enjoying what he was doing.

Bruce looked up at Vicki, and she flashed him a smile. Bruce understood the cue.

"Rachel, I think it is time for the flip," Bruce said

Rachel immediately turned over, and Bruce returned to rubbing her twat. This time, he could also use a free hand to massage her tits. At first, Rachel was shocked, not because she wanted Bruce to stop, but because it felt so damn good! Rachel feared that Greg would see Bruce rubbing her pussy and blow up. She looked over at her husband, fearful that he was watching, but he was still on his stomach with his head facing away. And Vicki! She was up on the table, sitting astride her husband's bare butt in all her hot nakedness. She watched as Vicki leaned forward, allowing her massive tits to drag along her husband's backside. When Vicki was fully stretched out, her naked body made continuous contact with Greg's body. Greg had to know what Vicki was doing and wasn't protesting. In fact, he seemed to be enjoying it. Therefore, why should she resist where Bruce touched her? So, she closed her eyes and let her mind drift to erotic thoughts. She thought how bad she was, but dam, it felt good.

It was now Greg's turn to turn over. He did so slowly, embarrassed by the raging boner he had. His dick was finally free, as it pointed straight up in the air. However, he was also shocked by the sight of his wife's body being ravaged by Bruce.

"Don't mind them, Vickie said," as she immediately went down on his cock.

Greg didn't know what to do. His wife was on the massage table while a muscular naked male masseuse with his hands all over her naked body. Including parts a legitimate masseuse would not touch. However, an equally nude female was sucking his erect dick, reminding him of his sexual desires. Greg could see his wife lifting her chest from the corner of his eye, forcing her right tit tight into Bruce's sucking mouth. Greg knew he should protest. But Vicki's warm wet mouth felt so good, caressing and sucking his dick.

In overt encouragement to Bruce's advances, Greg's wife started to stroke and rub his dick. Soon, it was fully erect. It seemed only fitting to Rachel as Vickie was sucking on her husband's dick at the other table. Vickie was licking Rachel's dick like a lollypop as she ran her tongue along the underside of Greg's dick, making it throb and ready to explode at any moment.

Greg looked over at his wife. Bruce was all over her body, fingers up her twat and rubbing her clit as he sucked on her tits. His wife was clearly enjoying herself as she thrashed about and let out moans of pleasure. He could see that she was also jacking Bruce's dick, and boy was he huge.

Vickie looked up and saw Greg watching Bruce and his wife go at it. "They seemed to be enjoying themselves. I think we should do the same." Vicki climbed up on the table with him and straddled Greg's hips. Her gaping pussy was directly above his twitching dick as her pendulous boobs swayed above his face.

Vickie clutched Greg's dick and positioned it between her outer pussy lips. Greg's mind was in turmoil. Should he speak up and say stop? However, as Vicki lowered herself slowly on his rock-hard dick, his dick said go, go, go. Soon he was halfway in the warm grasp of her pussy. Vicki continued lowering herself down on his dick until it became completely buried in her pussy's tight embrace. Vicki momentarily paused as she adjusted to the fullness of his big dick. Greg started to speak, not sure what to say. As he opened his mouth, Vickie inserted a boob into his mouth, preventing him from speaking. Vicky raised her hips and then lowered herself back down as she started fucking him. It wasn't long before Jim instinctively began thrusting his pelvis up in unison with Vick's downward motion. Greg had given in entirely to his lust and lost all signs of restraint. Soon he was pawing and caressing every part of Vicki's body as the two started fucking wildly.

Bruce knew it was his turn to go to the next step. Rachel's pussy was wet and obviously ready. Moving to the end of the table, Bruce grabbed Rachel under her knees. He then pulled her to the edge of the table. Lifting her legs, Bruce placed her feet on his shoulders. Bruce wasted no time as he spread her pussy lips with his fingers and positioned his dick at the entrance of her long-neglected pussy. Rachel did not protest as the tip of his giant dick teased her pussy, and Bruce thrust forward slowly. He knew he had to go slow, so the woman he was about to fuck could relax and adjust to the fullness of his giant dick.

Although the dick her husband was using on Vicki appeared to be just as big as his. Therefore, Rachel had experience in being fucked with a big dick. However, he nonetheless still needed to go slow. Soon, he was halfway in, then three-quarters, and finally all the way. Bruce paused for a moment, enjoying the warmness of her pussy, tightly grasping his dick. He then slowly started the rhythmic in and out of a couple fucking. Rachel responded by grabbing his butt and pulling him in deeper with every thrust. So deep he could feel his dick touch the entrance to her womb. Rachel couldn't help but think how Bruce's big cock was filling her pussy the way her husband did. Something she hadn't experienced in a long time. She was in heaven. Bruce, for his part, had the satisfaction of going balls deep into her pussy, with each inward thrust. Being fucked by his big dick was something many less experienced women couldn't take, and he would have to restrain himself so as not to cause any pain. However, Rachel was taking every inch of him and wanted more. With Rachel, he didn't have to hold back.

Over on the other table, her husband was oblivious to what his wife and Bruce were doing, as he was still fucking Vickie with wild abandonment. Greg hadn't fucked like this since his younger days when first fucking a new conquest, and like those times, he knew he wasn't going to last much longer. Suddenly Greg thrust his dick upward with maximum effort as his sexual energies went over the edge, releasing his cum. With deep thrusts, he instinctively tried to shoot its load as deep into Vicki's pussy as possible. With each thrust, he let out a loud moan of pleasure.

As he came down from his orgasmic high, Greg slumped into a restful peace. He rolled his head to the side and watched his wife being pounded by Bruce. Bruce was fucking her hard as his swing balls banged against her ass with each thrust. However, he couldn't protest as he had just drained his balls into Vicki's pussy, a pussy his withering cock was still inside. Greg watched as his wife grabbed Bruce's hips and pulled him in tight. It was apparent to Greg that his wife was beginning to come before his eyes with another man's dick deep in her pussy. Bruce, however, held off his orgasm. He wasn't finished pounding Greg's wife just yet.

Bruce slowed his pace until Rachel appeared to have completed coming. He then pulled out and turned Rachel over on her stomach. She had her feet on the floor and bent over the massage table. Bruce reentered her from behind and resumed fucking her hard, with fast and furious thrusts, deep into her pussy.

As Greg watched his wife continue to get fucked, Vicki climbed off his cock and grabbed a couple of wet towels from a towel warmer on the counter. She used one to wipe her pussy and the other to clean Greg's dick. Greg could see his wife coming again as her body stiffened, and Rachel gripped the table tightly. This time as she came, her pussy was squeezing down on Bruce's dick so hard he couldn't hold back any longer. Rachel let out loud, passionate moans as Bruce began pumping load after load of cum into her sex-starved pussy.

As Bruce pulled out of Rachel, Vicki went to open the door to tell Jane and Jim that they were finished with the massages. The shock of someone else possibly seeing what they had been doing brought Greg and Rachel out of their sexual trances. They both righted themselves and faced the door. Luckily, they were in a nudist resort and weren't expected to be dressed.

As she opened the door, Vicki was still wiping the cum from her crotch. Since Jane and Jim had been just outside the door, watching the show, Jane stepped in immediately, with Jim right behind.

"How were the massages?" Jane asked.

"Oh… the massages were just great," Rachel said, still trying to catch her breath.

Just then, a glob of cum drooled out of her pussy and ran down her thigh.

"I see Bruce gave you a massage, with a little extra at the end," Jane said. She then ran her finger across the tip of Bruce's still semi-erect dick, collecting some of its glistening juices before licking her finger clean.

"It ... is not what you think," Rachel said, searching for words, just then, more cum oozed from her pussy, and she quickly covered her crotch with her hands.

"Here," Vicki said, handing Bruce and Rachel some warm towels.

"How about some lunch?" Jim spoke up with a grin. Both Rachel and Greg were thankful for the change of subject.

Chapter 5 – Sit Here and Let's Talk

Greg and Rachel didn't talk much at lunch, and when they did speak, it was about how it seemed weird to be sitting in a restaurant naked with other couples eating lunch. However, no mention was made of what had just happened.

"Tonight, the resort will be a live band called the Bare Assets playing," Jane said, trying to keep the conversation going. "As you might guess by their name, the band plays in the nude. We will have a great time."

"I think I am ready to go home," Greg said.

"Are you sure? You're going to be missing an awesome band." Jim said, trying to persuade them.

"No. I think my husband is right," Rachel said. "You two can stay and enjoy the rest of your weekend. I think it is time for us to return to our room and get dressed."

"All right," Jane said. "We will walk back to our rooms with you."

When they returned, the door between the rooms was still open, and Jim and Jane entered Greg and Rachel's.

"Let's talk about what happened with Vicki and Bruce," Jane said.

"It was not what you thought." Greg snapped.

"Don't deny what happened," Jane continued. "When I asked if they could give you massages, they recognized you two as newbies. They also commented on how you checked out the other naked people at the resort. They also noticed the obvious boner Greg had going on."

"Before we left, Vicki flashed me a devious smile. We know Vicki and Bruce well and know they are as perverted as hell." Jane then leaned in and whispered in Greg's ear, but loud enough for Rachel to hear. "We know because the four of us have fucked together many times. So, we did what any equally perverted couple would do and peeked through the blinds to watch the show."

"You mean you watch us!" Rachel said, taken back by Jane's admission.

"Hell yeah! And watching you four go at it was as hot as hell. Both of you two were really going at it."

"Well, it had been a long time since the two of us had sex together, and I was caught up in the moment. I'm sorry, Rachel, forgive me." Greg said as he turned his attention to his wife.

"I thought you didn't want me," Rachel said.

"You never asked," Greg said. "I thought you didn't want me either. Then, this just happened. The thrill of having sex again and something wild and erotic like that was just too much to resist. I'm sorry I couldn't control myself."

"Well ... I must confess I enjoyed experiencing something new too," Rachel responded. "But aren't you mad that I cheated on you, Greg?"

"Just a minute, you two," Jane interjected. "Rachel, your husband's dick was just as buried in Vicki's twat as Bruce's dick was in yours. You were both enjoying yourselves immensely. Remember, we were spying on you, so don't deny it. I always say that a couple that plays together stays together."

"So, how would you two like to enjoy yet another new experience?" Jane said as she reached down again and gently took hold of Greg's dick. "Your dick looks like it would fill a girl's pussy nicely."

Greg looked over at his wife apprehensively. As he did, Jim approached Greg's wife from behind, cupped both her breasts, and gave them a little giggle. "Come on, old boy, you should share these treats, and while I am at it, you should check out what my wife has to offer."

Jane and Jim didn't wait for either to answer. Dropping to her knees, Jane immediately devoured Greg's cock, and Jim let his hands explore Rachel's body further. First, Jim lowered his left hand to Rachels's crotch and fingered her pussy. As he inserted his middle finger in her pussy, he avoided direct contact with her clit. First, he started to rub her love mound, then allowed his index finger to slide along the crevice between her outer pussy lips and thigh. At the same time, his little finger did the same on the other side. Then sliding his right hand over to Rachel's left boob, he hugged her tight and began to massage her tit while continuing to play with her pussy. Rachel leaned her head on Jim's shoulder as she got lost in the erotic sensations.

As Jane worked on his cock, Greg watched his wife being fondled by Jim. He could see that she was enjoying it, squirming her hips, trying to increase the pressure against Jim's probing hand. Greg decided to give in to his sexual desires and gently pulled Jane's head against his cock, forcing her to swallow more of his dick. Jane obliged as she grasped his butt cheeks. Greg's cock was growing by the second, soon filling Jane's mouth. Fortunately, being regulars at the Orange Blossom had given Jane plenty of experience with big cocks, as she could handle Greg's giant cock with little effort.

Jim could feel the spreading wetness on Rachel's pussy lips. Removing his hand from her pussy, he raised it to her mouth, and she sucked on his fingers, tasting her pussy juices. Jim then put his saliva-coated fingers back into her pussy with his fingers coated in her saliva. First, he slid his middle finger between her outer pussy lips before allowing it to pierce her moist hole. As he did that, he used his other hand to massage her boobs. Soon, Rachel thrashed about as his finger went in and out of her pussy, sliding along her engorged clit with every stroke.

His stiff cock was pressed in the crack of her butt cheeks as he kissed the nape of her neck. Jim thought she wanted him to go further but wasn't sure. There was only one way to find out: to go for it. Using one hand to hold her butt tight against him, he pushed her shoulders forward, causing her to lean over. As she did, she reached out to support herself off the bed.

Jim reached down and under her ass to finger her pussy from behind. As he did, she widened her stance to give him better access. No words were spoken, but Jim took this as an invitation to proceed. Jim ran his fingers of one hand through the folds of her moist pussy and gently spread the folds apart. Using his other hand, he positioned his rigid dick at the entrance to her fuck hole. If he had any doubt she wanted his cock, it was erased as she thrust her butt back on his member, burying him balls deep in her warm and wanting pussy. Jim didn't even have to move his hips as Rachel began to pull forward, then thrust backward on his dick. Jim just put his hands on her hips and enjoyed it. For extra stimulation, Rachel supported herself with one hand so she could use her free hand to finger her clit. Rachel was fucking in a wild frenzy. Jim looked down at Rachel's butt, and her pink little ass hole seemed to stare back at him. He reached out and ran his thumb across her butthole. Rachel jumped a bit at the unexpected sensation.

"Latter," Jim whispered. "But I will fuck you there before the weekend is over." Rachel looked over her shoulder and smiled in anticipation.

Greg watched the action and decided that if he was going to let Jim fuck his wife without him protesting, then it was only fair that he got to fuck Jim's wife. Besides, it wasn't as if he wasn't already engaging in sex with Jim's wife. They were both naked, and Jane had his dick down her throat. It was time for him to take it to the next level. Greg grabbed Jane under both shoulders and lifted her onto the bed as Jane raised her knees and spread her pussy lips with her fingers. Her pussy glistened with juices. She was ready and wanted Greg to fuck her. That was Greg's full intention, but not right away. Before he fucked her, he needed to suck on that sweet-looking pussy of hers. Her pussy had tempted him since they first got to the resort, and she stripped out of her clothes.

Greg dropped to his knees between her thighs and dove in. Not what Jane had expected, but what the hell? Anytime a guy wanted to eat her pussy, it was a good thing. Jane relaxed her thighs and gently pulled his face tight to her pussy. Greg lapped up her pussy juices, lost in the pungent smell of a woman's pussy. Greg thrust his tongue as deep into her pussy as he could, and when he needed to come up for air, he made sure to lick across her clit as he raised his head. Her pussy was just as sweet as Greg had imagined.

As she glanced over at her husband, Rachel was on the edge of coming. She was glad to see her husband was just as engrossed in Jane's pussy as she was being fucked by Jim. That was all Rachel needed to let herself go and thoroughly enjoy being fucked. She was soon going over the edge, having a thundering orgasm with all the mons of passionate sex. She clamped down hard on Jim's dick and continued wildly fucking her pussy as she came. Jim enjoyed this immensely but wanted it to last a little longer, so he held off coming. Greg's pussy eating seemed like a good idea. After Rachel finished orgasming, Jim pulled out and flipped her around. Rachel fell back onto the bed next to Jane, assuming the same position with her knees raised.

Jim went right to work, chowing down on Rachel's pussy. First, he licked up the overflowing pussy juices that escaped from her pussy while they were fucking. Then he explored the folds of her pussy lips before allowing his tongue to dart into her fuck hole. As Jim paid increasing attention to Rachel's inner deeps, she wiggled her hips to increase the sensation. Rachel let out a soft moan every time he raised slightly and flicked her clit with his tongue.

The two girls looked at each other, their faces only inches apart, as each had their pussy eaten by the other's husband. Rachel took the initiative to kiss Jane as if to thank Jane for helping her and Greg break out of their previous boring and sexless routine. Soon, both women were French kissing as they went into a sexual frenzy and came simultaneously.

As the girl's orgasms subsided, the guys both figured it was time for them to get themself off. Both guys raised up and impaled the other guy's wife with their dicks. Both pussies were wet and ready, and they slid in easily. Furiously they pounded the other guy's wife with their dicks. The girls were hanging on tight as both guys were going balls deep into their pussies, balls slapping against the girl's asses with every stroke.

Greg didn't take long to reach the point of coming, as he started moaning before his impending climax.

Jim slowed his pace as he and Rachel watched Greg's body stiffen and made a final hard thrust into Jane. Rachel especially watched intently as her husband came inside Jane. Greg moaned louder and thrust deeper as he tried to release his seed as deep into Jane's womb as he could. Greg's body then slumped as he finished.

Rachel seemed content. She couldn't get angry at her husband fucking another woman. After all, she had another guy's dick in her pussy, and he was picking up the pace. Jim was now fucking in and out of her with long fast strokes. Jim may have been the last to come, but he had been hard for a long time building up a massive load of cum. As he climaxed, he pumped load after load into Rachel's pussy, as her husband looked on.

The four relaxed for a while and talked about what had just happened.

After about an hour, Jane said, "I am getting hungry. Let's get a bite to eat. However, don't overeat. I don't want you guys to get too full that you don't want to fuck later." Said Jane said as she wiggled Greg's cock. I also want you two to see the Bare Assets Band. Let's shower and clean up first, though."

They all agreed that sounded like a good plan.

The shower was big enough for two, but they didn't shower with their spouses. Rachel and Jim went first. Rachel lathered up Jim, first paying particular attention to his genitals. Jim enjoyed that part as his dick began to stiffen. After rinsing Jim off, she bent down and gave his pecker a quick kiss.

It was now Jim's turn to wash Rachel. Standing behind her, the first place he started was her chest. Holding a boob in each hand, he couldn't resist giving her soapy jugs a slight giggle. As he did, he also kissed the nape of her neck. Jim was holding Rachel tight, and she could feel

Jim's still rigid dick in the crack between her butt cheeks. All this erotic contact affected Rachel, as she was getting horny and ready to go again.

Jim started to wash her backside and slid a soapy hand between her butt cheeks, allowing his fingers to slide to her pussy. As he ran his fingers through her lips, Rachel spread her stance to give him better access. Jim noticed her pussy lips felt moist and recognized the feeling as not merely from the shower water.

"You feel like you are ready to go again," Jim whispered in her ear.

"Maybe you should do something about that." She then leaned forward, bracing herself against the shower wall as he stuck her butt, pushing it against Jim's rigid dick.

She didn't have to tell Jim twice. His dick was already hard, and he promptly guided it into her wet and ready pussy. It wasn't long before they had fucked themselves into a frenzy, letting out all sorts of passionate sounds.

Jane and Greg heard the commotion and went to the bathroom. Opening the door, they stood at the entrance and watched the two of them fuck. It was a sight. Jim held onto Rachel's hips tightly as he fucked in and out of Rachel from behind, trying not to fall on the slippery floor. Rachel was grasping the towel racks to steady them both.

"I'm coming!" Rachel screamed as water cascaded down on the two of them. You would wonder why she had to announce that she was coming. Her facial expressions and moans of ecstasy made it quite apparent to the other three that she was having a massive orgasm.

"Do you want to do that when they are done?" Jane asked Greg with a smile.

"Hell yeah! Jim, hurry up and shoot your load into my wife so I can do the same with Jane."

Jim soon obliged as he shot his load into Rachel. After he finished coming, he paused, with his softening dick still inside Rachel. Then after pulling out and with water still cascading down on them, he washed the cum from her pussy and rinsed off his dick.

"Your turn, guys, and Greg, after you cum, make sure you clean my wife's pussy. I may want to have a snack tonight." Jim said as he stepped out of the shower and reached for some dry towels.

"And be quick about it. I am getting hungry." Rachel said as she followed Jim out of the shower and slapped her husband on his bare ass.

Chapter 6 – Getting into the Swing of Things

"You two are going to love the band playing tonight," Jane said as they finished their meals.

As they were getting tables over by the band stage, Vicki, Bruce, and Christian entered the opposite side of the room.

"Look, Jim, it's Vicki, Bruce, and Christian," Jane said as she motioned them to come over.

"Who is Christian?" Rachel whispered to Jane.

"Christian helps them at the Bare Essence Massage on the weekends.

"That boy is hung like a horse with muscles to match," Rachel said.

"That's nothing. You should see it when Christian dick is hard," Jane replied.

"You have had sex with him! He can't be more than twenty!"

"Yeah, I know," Jane replied with a smile.

"Hi, guys, good to see you again," Bruce said as he approached and shook Greg's hand. I would like you to meet Christian. Christian, meet Jim and Jane's new friends Greg and Rachel."

"Have a seat and enjoy the band with us. I am sure we can make room for the seven of us." Jim said.

Soon, the band began to play.

"Jane, you lied. The band members do have clothes on. She has boots on, he has a hat on, and most have belts on. They just don't have any pants on." Rachel said with a giggle.

"The two women our age are Ellen and Julie. Ellen is the one with the cowgirl hat and boots, and Julie is the one with the Amazon warrior look from a video game. April is the young girl in the hippie outfit. In the policeman's outfit is Ted, the bandleader, and the young drummer, dressed as a Roman gladiator, is Alex," Jane said.

Christian was sitting right next to Rachel as the band started to play. Rachel's mind was swirling with erotic thoughts. If Jane has had sex with Christian, could she, too? She imagined receiving a massage from Christian's firm hands and then finishing the massage with his big dick up her twat. Christian was at least 15 years younger, making her even horner. It would be like when she had sex back in her college days. Her pussy was getting wet at the thought. She tried to take her mind off Christian by looking around the room, but the room was full of naked guys everywhere she looked. Naked guys with her equipment on display. Young ones, old ones, tall ones, and small ones. Could she have sex with any of them? The two male band members captivated her as well. The older male band member was about her age, dressed like a police officer, and looked as sexy as hell. The drummer was the other male band member, and he was even younger than Christian, with a dick just as humungous. Looking around wasn't helping, but she didn't have to worry about Greg getting too jealous, or she would fire back at him, drooling at all the naked females in the room. He seemed to pay a lot of attention to the three female band members, two of which were about her age, one a big boobed brunet and the other more average-sized. The third female was young and petite, probably no more than 21. Rachel couldn't complain about Greg checking the young girl out since she was checking out the young drummer.

It wasn't long before Greg and Rachel were both into naked dancing. However, they didn't dance much with each other. Instead, they spend most of their time dancing with the others in the group. Greg found himself in several close dances with Vicki and Jane, where he started to get a hard-on as their tits rubbed up against his chest. And it wasn't long before Rachel began dancing a close dance with Christian. Rachel's mind exploded with erotic thoughts as Christian's mighty hand cupped her right ass cheek.

Greg and Rachel were both a bit relieved at the band's intermission. Rachel went to the women's room to wipe away the moisture that was collecting in her pussy, and Greg sat with his hands on his lap to cover his boner. As Rachel returned with a wiped-down twat, she and her husband were introduced to the band members.

"Glad to meet you," Ellen said. "Vicki tells me this is your first time at the Orange Blossom."

"Yes, this is our first time. Not only our first time here but also at a nudist resort." Rachel responded.

"So, how have you enjoyed yourself so far?" Julie asked.

"I can't speak for my wife, but I'm getting into this nudist thing," Greg said.

"Vicki tells me that's not all you have been into," Julie said with a coy smile and looked down at his dick.

Greg's face got red, and he didn't know what to say. The situation reminded him of when he got home extra late from a date on the night he lost his virginity. His dad asked how the date went and seemed to know what Greg had been doing.

"Don't be shy," Jane said, reaching down and grabbing his dick. "I did him soon after Vicki, and he defiantly got off enjoying himself."

"And Rachel, have you been enjoying yourself as well?" Julie asked.

"I see private gossip gets around fast here, so I suspect you know about Bruce, and I was with Jim afterward. I have no complaints." Rachel responded with a smile.

"Well, if that is the case, are you two up for a little more?" Ted asked.

"We are having a party in our room after tonight's show, and you are invited," Ellen said and glanced down at Greg's dick.

"We have a ton of snacks and drinks in our room," Jim said. "How about we have the party in our room?"

"If you insist," Ellen said. The rest agreed although Greg and Rachel were more reluctant and unsure of what they were getting into.

After the band went back to play their second set, Greg asked. "So, are we all going to be doing at this party, having sex like an orgy?"

The regulars all chuckled. "When the Bare Assets Band throws a party, it is a real fuck fest. You will definitely want to come if you want to screw," Jim said.

"He means cum, cum, and cum some more," Jane added.

After the band finished, Jim, Jane, Rachel, and Greg returned to Jim and Jane's room to get the snacks and drinks for the party. It wasn't long before the rest showed up, with Ellen carrying a large duffle bag.

The door wasn't even closed before Alex grabbed Rachel's butt, allowing his fingers to go almost to her butthole. Rachel jumped a bit. Did this young stud want to fuck her? Her pussy instantly watered at the thought.

"Slow down, tiger. I'm sure you will get to fuck Rachel soon enough," April said.

"Rachel, since you are a newbie here, I am sure all the guys will want to have a turn with you," Julie added. "And Greg, us girls want to go for a ride on that big dick of yours." She then reached out and grabbed his right butt cheek.

"Are you two up for that?" Jim asked.

Greg looked at his wife as if asking permission.

"I'm game if Greg's game," Rachel said. Who was she kidding? Her pussy was creaming at the thought of being fuck by five hot guys. Six, if her husband wanted to join in.

"Well, let's get to it," Greg said.

"Well, since you two are the center of attention and we have two beds in this room, Rachel, you go to that bed, and Greg, you take that one," Vicki said.

"I have some blindfolds," Ellen said. "How about we put them on you." She said as she retrieved them from her duffle bag without waiting for a response.

Greg and Rachel sat at the corner of their beds, nearest each other, as the blindfolds were secured, not sure what was in store for them next.

"Do you two want to take the kink level up yet another notch?" Julie asked.

"What do you have in mind," Greg asked.

"We have some restraints that will add even more excitement."

Because of the blindfold, Rachel could not see the shocked look on Greg's face, nor could he see her.

"Go for it!" An excited Rachel said.

"Rachel, don't you want to know more about this!" Her husband asked, slightly panicked.

"I'll show you what I have," Julie said. She then retrieved the restraints from the bag. They had multiple adjustable length straps and shorter Velcro straps for ankles and wrists at one end.

"Lift your blindfold slightly so you see what I got. The cuffs will loosely fit around your wrists. If you put hard your fingers together and hold them straight, you will be able to pull your hand out." Julie then demonstrated.

"We also have a safe word, which is 'RED.' Say red, and we stop. Understand?" Julie added.

"However, what are you going to do after that?" Greg asked.

"That's what the blindfold and restraints are for," April said with a smile. "We will figure it out as we go, and I'm sure you two will enjoy it."

"Oh, Greg, loosen up." His wife said. "This whole weekend has been a new adventure for you. So far, you got to screw Vicki and Jane. And I know you enjoy that. So, let's take a chance and see where this goes."

"But, we wouldn't see where it is going if we are blindfolded."

"Even better, we will be feeling our way through the unexpected. It sounds exciting." Rachel said as she leaned over, hugged her husband, and passionately kissed him.

"Okay, if you insist, but I am not entirely comfortable with this."

"That the old spirit, you won't regret it," Ted said.

The blindfolds and the restraints attached to their ankles and wrists were pulled back down over their eyes. Soon, Greg and Rachel were both spread eagle on their adjacent beds.

"Greg, they have got me spread-eagle over here on this bed. Rachel, how are you doing?"

"They have me spread-eagle as well. I feel like a piece of meat on display at a butcher shop. With my legs spread like this, my pussy is exposed, and I feel helpless. I'm sure all the guys are just staring at my wide-open pussy," Rachel said.

Suddenly, a hand grabbed her crotch, and a finger darted into her pussy. "That is the idea." A male voice said. "Now lift your butt so I can slide this pillow under you." Rachel wasn't sure, but she thought it was Jim.

"Lift your butt so that we can put a second pillow under you."

Rachel's hips were now arched, her thighs wide apart, and her pussy was jutting up to give the guys full access.

Without warning, a hand grabbed Greg's dick. "You do the same, big fella." Greg heard a female voice, possibly Julie, say. "Come on, lift your butt." As he did, three pillows were stuffed under him as well.

"Now, some guy is between my legs and is licking my pussy! I think it's Ted." Rachel said as she tried to wiggle her hips to increase the contact.

"Shit, someone is sucking my cock." It was Ellen, but he didn't know who it was, as she never spoke.

"You two need to stop talking so much. Here, eat my pussy," April said as she sat on Greg's face.

"The same for you." Rachel was told as a giant cock landed on her face. "Open up and suck my dick," Christian said.

"Ted," Alex asked, "let me have a taste of her pussy before Christian fills it with cum."

Rachel squirmed her hips as Alex dove in and immediately stuck his tongue deep into her twat.

Greg's dick was rock hard as Ellen deep-throated his dick. Suddenly she stopped, raised up, and impaled herself on his dick. As she did, April leaned forward and started sucking on her tits.

"Rachel is ready for you, Christian," Alex said as he stopped sucking her pussy.

Who was he kidding? She was ready as soon as she was tied up, and Alex just wanted an excuse to eat her pussy.

If there was doubt that she was ready, it was eliminated as Christian's big dick slid in easily. Rachel took him all, as Christian was balls deep in her pussy and pounding away in no time.

Greg's and Rachel's bodies were simultaneously fucked and molested by multiple people. Guys that couldn't access Rachel stood nearby, jacking rigid dicks, waiting their turn. Similarly, the girls who weren't fucking Greg or having their pussies eaten sat around in chairs, legs splayed, fingering their clits. They wanted to keep themselves on the verge of coming when it was their turn.

Greg's senses were on overload. His dick was in one pussy as another was in his face. He could hear sucking sounds above him as April sucked Ellen's tits, and the air was full of the scent of hot pussy. He was on the verge of coming.

"Don't let him come, Ellen! We all want turns on his dick," Julie said.

Ellen stopped and raised up, pulling his dick from her pussy, and immediately grabbed the base of his dick and pushed her thumbs into the underside, stopping his urge to come.

After a short pause, Julie mounted his dick and started fucking away. April then returned to riding Greg's face and sucking boobs, this time Julie's boobs.

Rachel started to let out moans of an imminent orgasm as she did, her pussy clamped down on Christian's dick. This sent him over the edge as he pumped a massive load of cum deep into her pussy.

"Oh my God, oh my God!" Rachel screamed as Christian groaned with each spasm of his dick. As soon as Christian was finished coming, he rolled off her, and her cum filled pussy was immediately filled with another dick, this time Ted's.

Greg realized that Christian had just come inside his wife's pussy, and she had an orgasm. If that was the case, he figured it was his turn. His dick was throbbing and ready to explode. However, before he could come, whoever was fucking him rose, letting his dick come out of the pussy his dick was in, and that thumb pressure was back at the base of his dick. Suddenly another pussy slid down his dick. Oh, it gripped his dick hard. It was a tight little pussy.

April was in a frenzy. She was already on the verge of coming from having Greg eat her pussy. She frantically humped up and down. Suddenly, they both exploded in orgasmic tremors. Greg pumped what seemed to be an endless amount of cum into April's tight little twat.

Over on Rachel, Ted came and was immediately replaced by Alex and another giant dick stuffing her pussy.

"Your husband got my pussy all messy. Clean it up!" April said as she sat on Rachel's face.

Rachel had come to expect dick after dick in her pussy. But a cum filled pussy in her face! Rachel wasn't ready for that and her own husband's cum at that!

Rachel froze as the cum dripped from April's cunt and onto her face.

"Start sucking the cum out of my pussy!" April demanded as she rubbed her cum drenched pussy in Rachel's face.

Rachel started licking, not sure how she was to do it. April didn't care much about her technique so long as Rachel licked up the cum. Ultimately, she licked up half of her husband's cum, and the other half was on her face, nose, and chin.

Alex leaned forward as he continued to fuck Rachel and took one of April's small tits into his mouth.

Rachel was starting to get into pussy licking as she let her tongue explore the inner depths of April's pussy. With Alex sucking her tits and Rachel's tongue up her twat, April was ready to come again. Her body shook as she had a second climax. Alex now lost it, filling Rachel's pussy with her fourth load of cum. Rachel's pussy was overflowing with cum, running out and down across her butthole and onto the pillow below. Alex was still driving his big dick hard and deep into Rachel's pussy as he emptied his ball, sending her into another orgasm.

Over at Greg's bed, things were a little slower. Jane was busy sucking cum and pussy juice off Greg's withering dick. There was no way he was ready to fuck, and Jane was getting impatient, wanting her turn to ride Greg's dick!

"Prostate massage, we need a prostate massage!" Jane announced.

Prostate massage, what the hell was that? Greg thought to himself.

Before he knew what was happening, female hands were all over his body. His ankle straps had been removed, and his knees pushed up against his chest. Soon he was strapped down in this position, with his butt sticking up in the air. He felt uneasy, and his dick was getting limper, not harder.

That was about to change!

He felt two hands pulling his butt cheeks apart. Then something cold was squirted on his butthole. Lube! A finger started to smear the lubricant around. Then a slender finger slipped into his butthole.

"He is ready. Give me the big dildo."

"What!"

That wasn't the safe word. Jane smeared a generous amount of lube on its tip, positioned the big plastic dick at the hole where things were supposed to come out, and pushed the dildo in. In doing so, the dildo pushed against his prostate on the other side of his anal wall. Now Greg remembered what the prostate was. The internal male sex organ produces seaman and produces a male's ejaculation.

"Oh, shit, that hurts!" Greg screamed.

"Are you okay, Greg? His wife asked, not able to see what was going on.

Greg paused for a second as the shock wore off. "I'm fine, honey. But I just got a dildo the size of a telephone pole stuck up my ass, that's all."

"Better you than me."

Several of the others in the room looked at each other and smiled.

The dildo did the trick, as Greg's dick almost instantly got hard.

The girls quickly rearranged the straps and put Greg back into a spread-eagle position. But they left the dildo up his ass!

Jane quickly mounted his still-rigid dick and started fucking. It wasn't long before she came. Having cum several times earlier in the day and just recently in April, Greg could hold off coming this time. When Jane finished coming and got off his dick, Vicki quickly took her place on his still rigid fuck stick.

Over on Rachel's bed, Bruce was pounding her sloppy twat. Soon he pumped even more cum into the overflowing pussy. So far tonight, Rachel had taken five loads of cum. Bruce pulled out, and his cum, poured out of her pussy, and down to her ass. She could feel it between her butt cheeks as it ran down.

As Vicki fucked Greg, Ellen squeezed between Greg's legs to suck his ball, occasionally stopping to lick the base of his shaft as they fucked. Soon, Greg and Vicki started explosive orgasms as Greg shot hot streams of cum into Vicki. As their bodies trembled in their climaxes, Ellen kept licking up the cum and cunt juices running out of Vicki's twat.

"Now what?" Christian asked as he stroked his rejuvenated monster cock. "I'm ready to go again."

All the guys in the room, except her husband, had taken turns fucking Rachel, pumping five loads of cum into her pussy. Rachel was still tied down, spread eagle, with globs of cum drooling out of her fuck hole and down onto the pillow under her butt. Christian, Tim, and Jim were all massaging hard-ons, ready for another round.

"I say we use the other hole this time," Jim said. "Everyone grab either an arm or a leg."

Oh, SHIT, Rachel thought. She knew what that meant and wasn't sure she was ready for that! But she was afraid to say anything else.

"I think it's your turn to get something stuck up your ass, or should I say things." Her husband chuckled.

Jim and Christian then flipped her butt up, with her hip on the cum covered pillows. This time her wrists were strapped to her ankles, causing her butt to stick up in the air. Two straps were still used to keep her legs spread and prevent her from sliding up to the head of the bed as she got fucked. The pillows between her thighs would have given her some comfort ... if they hadn't been cum covered. In this position, her butt stuck up in the air, and her cheeks were slightly spread, giving the guys a clear view of her pink butthole.

"I think she is ready," Alex said, then slapped her ass without warning.

"Ouch!" Rachel screamed.

"Ewww," Alex said, not realizing her ass was covered in cum scum. He then wiped his hand off her back.

"Are you okay, honey?" Greg asked.

"I'm okay. It was just a little-unexpected slap on my ass."

WAMM. "Enough of the chit-chat," Ellen said after leaving her handprint on Greg's left butt cheek. Ellen went back to sucking Greg's cock clean. It was her turn to fuck Greg next. She had been the first to fuck Greg that night but had to stop before she came, fearing he would come too soon. This time, she wanted to get herself off and needed him hard again.

Jim got some lube and spread a liberal amount around Rachel's butthole. Rachel nervously anticipated what would happen next. She knew she was about to get it in the ass, that much she knew. But she had never had anal sex before and did not know what to expect. It wasn't that she was opposed to the idea. She always wanted Greg to try it but was too embarrassed to ask. She knew she was going to find out soon what it was like. It appeared that Jim would be her first. The thought of Jim possibly going first put her a little at ease. First, she trusted him to go slow. Second, he had a shorter dick than the other guys. Not that it was small, just she wasn't ready to take on Christians or Alex's giant ramrods.

Rachel jumped a little when Jim popped a finger into her butt. Jim pulled his finger out, put some more lube on it, and finger fucked her some more.

"She is really tight, guys," Jim said. "Give me a medium-size dildo with plenty of lube so I can loosen her up."

Jim took the dildo and slowly worked it into her butt. When it was halfway, he wiggled it side to side before beginning to fucking her butt in and out. As he fucked her butt with the dildo, Jim used a free hand to squirt more lube on his dick.

Jim jacked his rigid dick several times to spread the lube before pulling the dildo out of her butt. Before her butthole had an opportunity to close, he stuck the tip of his hick into the open hole. Slowly, Jim pushed forward, and soon, his dick was all the way up Rachel's butt.

"Relax," Jim whispered as he paused for a moment to give her time to get used to the fullness.

Jim pulled out slightly before thrusting back in equally slowly. He slowly started to fuck her with increasingly longer strokes. At the same time, he kept the pace slow and steady.

"I told you I would fuck you in the ass before the weekend was over," Jim whispered in her ear.

As Rachel began to relax, Jim picked up the pace. However, he couldn't last much longer, as the tightness of her butt was too much for him to take, causing him to explode and release a torrent of cum into her bowels.

After Jim finished coming, he pulled out of her butt, and Ted's dick immediately filled her hole. Rachel was okay with that, as he was about the same size as Jim. Like Jim, Tim didn't last long, as he quickly came and sent another load up her ass. Rachel was starting to enjoy this. Ted paused for a moment as he finished climaxing, then rolled off her.

"SHIT!" Rachel screamed as Christian entered her with his giant dick. Oh god, he was big. Lucky for her, he was going slow. But the pain was still excruciating. Like the guys before him, Christian didn't last long and pumped another load into her ass. Rachel felt relieved as she felt him coming. As he pulled out, her asshole was gaping, and cum poured out. It was Alex's turn next. After three guys, including Christian's giant dick, Rachels's ass was fully stretched. She took Alex's equally big dick with a fair degree of ease.

Over on Greg's bed, Ellen had been licking and sucking his dick for some time. While she did, Julie was behind her with her face buried in Ellen's ass, eating Ellen's pussy from behind. Ellen was ready to come at any moment but wanted Greg's dick hard and up in her twat when she did. Greg's dick was getting stiffer, but it still wasn't quite ready. Ellen then grabbed the dildo still stuck up his ass and worked it in, out, and around a bit. Greg groaned as his dick became stiffer. Ellen wasted no time and quickly moved up and mounted herself on his giant member.

Julie then moved forward to take Ellen's place. She grabbed the dildo with one hand and Greg's balls with the other. Greg's mind was a swirl of pain and pleasure as Ellen humped his dick fast and furiously. Soon Ellen was over the orgasmic edge as she fingered her clit while fucking Greg.

Christian came, and Bruce was next. Bruce was smaller and easily entered Rachel's stretched and cum filled ass. Rachel recounted the number of times she had been fucked. First, five guys fucked her in her pussy, and then four fucked her in the ass. All of them had come, pumping her full of cum. And now Bruce was in her ass, probably the last. Bruce was going slow and easy.

Damn, this was starting to feel good, Rachel was thinking. But wait, what was this? She heard the humming sound of a vibrator, then a soft feminine hand softly touching her left boob, probably a female's. It was Jane, and she had the vibrator. As Bruce fucked Rachel in the ass, Jane inserted the vibrator into Rachel's swollen, neglected, and overheated pussy.

"Oh, my God," Rachel said as she was being fucked in both holes.

Over on Greg's bed, after Ellen finished coming, she was replaced by Julie on his dick. Someone else took over the big dildo up his ass. Greg didn't know who it was, but they were gentler and left his balls alone.

It was Julie who was fucking Greg with long steady strokes. God damn, he was in heaven.

Both Rachel and Greg could feel a huge orgasm building.

Greg started to cum first. "Ah, Ahh, Ahhhh!" Greg moaned as his orgasm built. Greg tried to thrust, but the restraint strap prevented him from moving. Julie maintained a slow, steady pace. Greg's orgasm seemed endless as Julie continued to fuck him slowly.

Just then, the dildo was suddenly thrust deep into his ass. "Shit!" Greg screamed as he shot spasm after spasm of cum into Julie. Julie suddenly clutched Greg tightly as she came herself.

Greg's orgasm seemed endless. The giant dildo was pulled from his ass just as he was finished coming. Rachel didn't get off Greg immediately as she laid on top of Greg until his withering dick plopped out of her pussy. Rachel then rolled off to his side, and April crawled between his legs to suck his spent dick clean as the other girls removed his blindfold and restraints.

Greg then rolled on his side and watched his wife as she came in a thundering orgasm. Her body struggled against the restraints as she shook. Bruce also started to climax, pumping yet another load of cum into her ass.

After Bruce finished pumping his cum into her ass, Rachel was untied and her blindfold removed. Rachel was helped off the bed and found herself facing her husband. She realized that her husband had watched Bruce fucking her in the ass. Rachel was an embarrassed fucked-up mess. She had received ten loads of cum, two each for five different guys. A river of Cum was pouring out of her crotch and ass and running down her thighs. She covered her crotch to prevent more cum from pouring out. There was more cum on her belly and back from laying on the cum soaked pillows. She even had cum on her face when she had to lick it out of April's pussy. Her own husband's cum, from another woman's pussy at that.

Rachel looked down at her filthy body as if in shame, then looked up at her husband. "Do you still love me?" She asked, fearful of the answer.

Greg didn't say anything as he reached out, hugged her tight, and gave her a passionate kiss, oblivious to all the cum on her face. They then quietly walked arm and arm to the shower in their room.

Jim and Jane were exhausted as they looked at their disheveled beds, covered in fuck juices. They decided to go to Greg's and Rachel's room to use one of their clean beds as the others returned to their rooms.

In the shower, Greg and Rachel slowly washed each other's bodies. Greg gently caressed his wife's pussy as he washed out the cum with the handheld shower, and his wife paid equal attention to his dick and balls.

After toweling each other off, they went to the open bed across from Jim and Jan and laid together in the spoon position. Greg kissed and caressed his wife, oblivious to Jim and Jane. Greg didn't care if they watched, although it didn't matter, as Jim and Jane were exhausted from their sexcapades and had fallen asleep.

Soon Greg's dick became hard as he fingered his wife's pussy. In this position, he could position his big long dick at the entrance to her fuck hole. Rachel raised her leg a little to give him better access from behind, and they started to slowly fuck. Both came quietly and fell fast asleep without moving from the spoon position.

Chapter 7 – Check Another Off the Bucket List

Greg heard running water and rustling sounds as he rubbed the sleep from his eyes. His wife was still asleep in his arms.

"Good morning, stud." He heard Jane say.

Jane and her husband Jim were naked, standing before him, toweling off from their morning showers. Greg closed his eyes briefly and reopened them, still in a bit of a morning grog. Yep, a naked female was casually toweling off in front of him while his naked wife was in his arms. Wow, how his life had changed in just 24 hours.

The added commotion caused Rachel to wake up as well. She was pleased that she was still lying in her husband's arms, with his dick pressed into the crack of her ass. It was just as she remembered before falling asleep.

"Are you two sleepy heads ready for some breakfast?" Jim asked

For the rest of the morning and early afternoon, Greg and Rachel acted like a couple of newlyweds, always holding hands and frequently kissing. They ate breakfast with Jim and Jane and went canoeing, hiking, and other activities.

Later, they lounged in the hot tub with Jim, Jane, and another couple as jets of hot water created a frothy swirl around their naked bodies. As Greg and Rachel sat close together, Jim and Jane chatted with the other couple. Greg and Rachel quietly kept to themselves.

When the Bare Assets Band started their afternoon pool party, Jim asked, "Let's get a seat closer to the band before they're all taken. We will have to check out of the resort in a couple of hours, and this will be the last chance to hear the band before we leave."

The other couple in the hot tub quickly hurried out to get a good seat.

"Jim and Jane, I think I would prefer to relax here in the hot tub for our last few hours," Greg answered as he put his arm around his wife.

"You two go on. We can still hear the band, okay, over here." Rachel said as she cuddled closer to her husband.

Jim and Jane left, and Greg and Rachel found themself alone in the hot tub.

It didn't take Rachel long before her hand found her husband's dick and began stroking it.

"What are you doing? There are people all around." Greg said in a low voice.

"No one can see a thing below these bubbles. Besides, they all have their backs to us, listening to the band."

Rachel continued stroking his dick, which soon gave her the desired response.

"I'm not sure about this, Rachel. There must be 100 people over there listening to the band. What if they see us?"

"That's the challenge we are going to have. We will have to be slick about it. I always fantasized about being tied up and gangbanged by a bunch of horny guys, which happened last night. They also did anal on me, another fantasy. Now I can cross them off my bucket list."

"That anal it wasn't a one-time thing, was it? You and I never did that. I mean, can I try that with you sometime?"

"Of course, we can, and I promise soon. However, right now, I want to check another thing off my bucket list, to fuck in public."

"One of the things that I have also learned this weekend is that I need to be more open about my own wants and needs. Now lift me up and lower me down on your lap while I guide your dick into my pussy."

"Okay, but we best not be caught."

Greg put his hands up under her shoulders to lift her up. Added by the buoyancy of the water, he was able to easily lift her up as Rachel guided his dick into pussy, as she settled down on his lap. After a short pause, she slowly bobbed up and down on her husband's dick.

About 20 feet away, an old lady turned around and looked their way. Rachel immediately froze.

"Put your arms around me and act like you're holding me tight."

"I love the music the band is playing," Rachel said loud enough for the lady to hear.

The lady looked at them suspiciously, then turned back towards the band.

"Keep your arms around my waist. It looks more innocent that way." Rachel said as she returned to humping his dick.

A little later, the lady turned around to check on them again.

This time, Rachel stopped more quickly and smiled at her, and the old lady promptly turned back around.

Greg and Rachel went back to fucking. This time the lady left them alone long enough for Greg to shoot his load, and Rachel could feel Greg's dick spasming and shooting his cum into her pussy.

Rachel smiled. She did not come, as there would be time for that later. Rachel was content with the knowledge of making her husband happy and that she had just fucked in public, and she could now check that one off her bucket list as well.

Rachel slid off Greg's lap, then rubbed her pussy to get the cum out as the water jets quickly washed away the evidence of their sex.

Jim and Jane returned from the band performance.

"You missed a good show. The band was really getting into it," Jane said.

"We were getting into it too, especially Greg," Rachel said and reached down and gave Greg's dick a wiggle.

Jim and Jane both smiled, knowing what she meant.

"Unfortunately, it's checkout time, and we must put our clothes on," Jim said.

"So, will you two want to come back again?" Jane asked.

"Maybe, but only for the nudist experience," Rachel said.

"So, you didn't enjoy the sex?" Jane asked.

"Oh, don't get us wrong," Greg said. "We both enjoyed the new sexual experiences and checked off several items on our bucket list. But Rachel and I have decided that having sex with others is not our thing. However, hanging out in the nude has been great fun, and we want to do that more. And... I will need a tennis partner."

Thank you for reading!

Please review - W.E. Sinful

Other books in the Orange Blossom Series

Jim and Jane Become Nudist: Readers are introduced to Jim and Jane and follow them as they become nudists. First, they go to a topless beach, then nude beaches, and finally, the Orange Blossom, enjoying sexual benefits along their journey. At first, they are afraid to tell anyone but eventually confide in their best friend, Debbie, who joins them on nude beach trips.

Debbie Wants to Go: After their first trip to the Orange Blossom nudist resort, Debbie is taken by Jim and Jane's description and the band that plays in the nude. Jane then asked if she wanted to join them on their next trip to the Orange Blossom. Debbie eagerly agrees and does the Orange Blossom in a big way as she releases her pent-up sexual desires.

The Bare Assets Band: Readers are introduced to the band that plays in the nude. The group started as a regular nightclub five-piece. Still, they had to overcome their modesty when the financial need required them to accept an offer to play at the Orange Blossom Nudist Resort. They end up doing much more than merely becoming nudists...

Other books by W.E. Sinful

The Mars Club: An erotic space adventure about mankind's first landing on Mars. The adventure begins on Earth as the candidates compete for flight team positions. If you think joining the Mile-High Club sounds exciting, you will want to join... *The Mars Club!*

The Payton Inn series: The Payton Inn is a resort hotel in Orlando, Florida. Oh, if these walls could speak, is a common phrase, and oh, the stories they could tell. Read the series and learn about the hot sexual escapades at the ... *The Payton Inn.*

Also by W.E. Sinful

The Orange Blossom Nudist Resort
Jim & Jane Become Nudist - Would You Dare to Bare? - Book 1 of the
Orange Blossom Series
The Bare Assets Band - What Would You Do for Money? - Book 3 of
the Orange Blossom Series
Debbie Wants to Go - Book 2 of the Orange Blossom Series
The Orange Blossom Nudist Resort - Would You Bear It All?
What Did You Do This Weekend?

The Payton Inn
Bachelor Party Two Different Parties Two Different Endings from the
Payton Inn Series
Birthday Present for Jeffery from the Payton Inn Series
Getting Revenge and Then Some from the Payton Inn Series - If You
Have Ever Been Cheated on You Will Want to Read about Grace and
Hudson's Revenge
Mia Goes Hooker Spotting (Includes Second Bonus Story) from the
Payton Inn Series
New Thrill Addison & Val Try Escorting
Ruby from the Payton Inn Series
Teach Me ... Teach Me Everything
The Payton Inn 12 Stories from the Payton Inn Series

Threesome - Every Mans Fantasy - From the Payton Inn Series

Standalone
The Mars Club - And You Thought the Mile-High Club Was the Club
to Join